The Adventures of Capitol Kitty

An Almost True Story

by **SHARON DAVIS**

illustrations by **DANIEL SAN SOUCI**

To my parents, Don and Mary Ryer,

who brought the joy of reading into my life,

and to the children of California — may they know the same joy.

— S.D.

ISBN 0-439-45069-1

Library of Congress Cataloging-in-Publication Data Available

10 9 8 7 6 5 4 3 2   02 03 04 05 06

Book design by Elizabeth B. Parisi

Printed in Mexico   49
First Scholastic printing, October 2002

The Adventures of Capitol Kitty is based on a real cat who lives at the California State Capitol in Sacramento. This whimsical tale was created to help young people get a sense of who works in the capitol as well as to provide lessons about friendship, truthfulness, and courage.

As the First Lady of California, I visit schools throughout the state and have the opportunity to meet with students, parents, and educators. I have seen firsthand that reading is a gateway skill and a fundamental building block of academic success. If students are going to become confident learners, they must first become confident readers. That is why the Governor and I created the Governor's Book Fund.

The Governor's Book Fund is a nonprofit program established to provide monetary grants to California elementary, middle, and high schools for the purchase of library books. The prime mission of the Fund is to develop private sector resources to increase literacy and enhance the pleasure of reading for all Californians. We know reading skills are significantly improved when students have access to a wide selection of informational, entertaining, and up-to-date books.

I am pleased to work with California State Librarian Dr. Kevin Starr and the California State Library Foundation, which administers the Fund. Both have a long history of supporting statewide literacy initiatives and educational programs. All author proceeds from the sale of this book and related merchandise go directly to the Governor's Book Fund to benefit school libraries.

The Governor and I are focused on improving schools, increasing resources in education, and ensuring that every child in California learns to read. On behalf of the state and the citizens of California, I thank you for your support of this resource program and for your efforts to bring a future full of possibilities to our next generation through the joy of reading.

Scholastic Inc. shares our commitment to provide young people with greater access to literature, and I am pleased to partner with them on this project. I hope you enjoy meeting Capitol Kitty and find her adventures as inspiring as I have.

Sharon Davis

Capitol Kitty lived under a windowsill, behind the bushes in front of a large stone building that just happened to be the State Capitol of California. All day long, Capitol Kitty watched over her kingdom. All the flower beds, monuments, and trees that surrounded the capitol building were part of her kingdom. Every morning and every night, Capitol Kitty stood in her special spot near the entrance of the capitol, greeting all the employees like a queen reviewing her royal subjects.

One day as she was enjoying her dinner, Capitol Kitty was distracted by a strange sound coming from a nearby flower bed. At first she ignored it, but the meow-hoo-hoo-hoo just wouldn't stop.

It didn't take long for Capitol Kitty to find a skinny little cat crouching low in a flower bed. The strange cat was too busy crying to hear Capitol Kitty approach. He jumped when Capitol Kitty said, "What's all this noise about? Stop that immediately!"

The cat wrapped his paws around his ears as the tears rolled down his cheeks and onto his droopy whiskers. He meow-hoo-hooed even louder and trembled so much that even the flowers around him shook.

Capitol Kitty softened her voice. "I'm not going to hurt you," she said. "Tell me why you are making so much noise, and maybe I can help you."

The cat looked at Capitol Kitty with sad, teary eyes and said in a shaky voice, "Some alley cats pounced on me and chased me. I ran and ran until I was too tired to run anymore. And now you'll probably make me go away, too. Meow-hoo-hoo-hoo."

Capitol Kitty wanted to keep Capitol Park all to herself, but she didn't want to act like those mean alley cats. How could she get rid of her unwelcome guest?

Capitol Kitty thought and thought. Finally, she came up with a plan. If she took the young cat into the capitol building, they would be chased out immediately. Then the scared little cat would run far, far away. And Capitol Kitty would have the park all to herself again.

Capitol Kitty offered the scrawny cat some of her food and asked, "Do you have a name?"

The little cat looked down at the ground. "I don't have a name or a home. I just run from place to place. I'm scared of everything — that's why they call me Scare D Cat. But you can call me D Cat," he added shyly, "if you want to."

"Then that's what I'll call you. And you can call me Capitol Kitty."

"Why do they call you that?" asked D Cat.

"Don't you know where you are?" asked Capitol Kitty proudly, puffing out her chest. "This is the capitol of the great state of California and a very important place. It has been here for more than 130 years, and there has always been a cat to watch over the park. And now I am the Capitol Kitty."

"I've seen lots of big buildings. Why is the capitol so important?" asked D Cat.

"This building is the government house for the state. All of the important work of the state is done here by representatives who have been elected by the people," Capitol Kitty began to explain. Then she remembered her plan.

"Why don't I show you around?"

"You mean we can go inside?" D Cat asked in amazement.

"Of course. Just follow me." Together, the two cats walked right up to the door. There were so many people leaving that it was easy to scurry in.

Just as Capitol Kitty had planned, the capitol police officer stationed near the door shouted, "Hey, you cats don't belong in here. Out! Out!"

But instead of running outside, far, far away, D Cat bolted up the stairs. Totally surprised, Capitol Kitty ran after him. The police officer chased after the cats shouting, "Stop!"

On the second floor, D Cat ran to the end of the hall and slid across the waxed floor right into a large chamber, followed by Capitol Kitty and the police officer.

It was the state assembly chamber. The assembly members were voting on a bill that could become a law. The cats and the police officer ran through the green-carpeted chamber between the antique desks. Papers flew, people shouted, and someone pounded a gavel to try to bring the chamber to order.

D Cat led Capitol Kitty out a side door, then continued down another hall. More police joined the chase, and so did a specially trained police dog.

The long hall led to the other side of the capitol building and the state senate chamber. The senators were inside listening to an important speech when the two cats burst into the room, followed by the police and their dog. The cats ran under a row of desks, knocking into the legs of confused senators. The senators lifted their feet in surprise. Afraid to stop, Capitol Kitty just followed D Cat. When they reached the last desk, they leaped onto an empty chair, then over a railing, and out the back door, somehow managing to escape!

The police were shouting. The police dog was barking. The chase continued down the staircase and into the main corridor of the capitol.

The cats were both so scared they ran through a set of large double doors. Surely, this was the way out!

But as soon as they went through them, Capitol Kitty realized they had gone the wrong way again. With the police and the dog so close on their tails, there was no turning back. As the cats raced through the office, assistants yelled and scrambled out of their way. Finally, they entered a large office with a long table surrounded by important-looking people.

Just as the police were about to grab the cats, Capitol Kitty and D Cat jumped onto the long table and slid all the way to the end, landing in the lap of the governor! The governor leaped out of his seat in surprise, and the cats tumbled to the floor. They scrambled to their feet and raced out the door, just as the governor's security officers joined the others in the chase.

The cats dashed under the staircase and into a nearby janitor's closet. They crouched down low, holding their breath as they heard the police, the dog, and the security officers running up the stairs to the second floor.

"Do you see the trouble you got us into?" Capitol Kitty said in a huff.

"Me? You're the one who said we could come inside!" replied D Cat.

Capitol Kitty remembered her plan. "You're right." She paused. "I thought I could scare you away and have Capitol Park all to myself again."

D Cat's head hung low. "I thought you were different from the other cats. I thought you were special. Now I see that you're just as mean as the rest of them."

Capitol Kitty looked away, embarrassed. She had always thought of herself as special. The people who worked at the capitol treated her like she was different from other cats. But she didn't feel very special now. She thought about it for a moment and said in a quiet voice, "I'm sorry. I never should have tried to send you away."

D Cat stayed silent.

Capitol Kitty tried again. "You know, you did a pretty good job of getting away from the police and that pesky dog. You have a real talent for getting around."

D Cat pouted. "So I can run from place to place. What good is that?"

"Did you know," asked Capitol Kitty, "that there have always been great explorers and that is just what they do? They go from place to place, discovering new things and finding new places."

"How can I trust you after what you just did to me?" asked D Cat, still upset.

"Isn't there anything I can say that will make you trust me again?" asked Capitol Kitty.

D Cat shook his head stubbornly.

Capitol Kitty was silent for a moment. Then she said, "Well then, I'll just have to prove it to you. We'll go as soon as it's safe."

When the capitol was finally quiet, Capitol Kitty pushed open the door and said, "Come on, I have something to show you." D Cat followed her cautiously.

The two cats crept through the dark building. Finally, they came to a large room under a high dome. In the center stood a giant statue of a man kneeling next to a woman in a long gown.

Capitol Kitty pointed to the statue. "That man is an explorer named Christopher Columbus," she said. "He's asking Queen Isabella of Spain for permission to travel and discover new places. What he did was very special. Even though he lived more than five hundred years ago, children still learn about him in school."

D Cat looked up at the statue in astonishment. He stayed there for a long time, thinking about the great explorer and imagining his adventures.

Once the cats were back outside and under the protection of the bushes, Capitol Kitty quickly went to sleep. But D Cat stayed awake all night, thinking about what had happened.

By the time the sun came up, D Cat had made a decision. It was time for him to go. And, for the first time, he wasn't afraid — he was excited about all the new things in the world to see and do. He would be an explorer.

"Before I go, I think I need a new name. What do you think of the name Traveler?" he asked Capitol Kitty.

"I like it," she said. "It suits you." By now, Capitol Kitty was a little sad to see the young cat go. "Will you promise to come back and tell me all about your travels?"

"Of course I will," said Traveler. "But no more tours of the capitol."

"Agreed!" said Capitol Kitty.

Capitol Kitty watched Traveler march across the wide lawn and out into the world. She had the capitol all to herself again, but she was going to miss her new friend.

Soon she heard the people arriving for work at the capitol. Quickly, Capitol Kitty scurried to her special place near the entrance and settled in to once again watch over her kingdom.